Who Uses This?

by Margaret Miller

Greenwillow Books, New York

I would like to thank all of the following children, grown-ups, and organizations whose patience, generosity, and good humor made this book possible: Allan Kerr, Sabrina Steel, Rebecca Chace, Sam Spector, the Columbia University Department of Athletics, Michael Fusco, Diana Lizardi, Sylvia Roberts, the Bank Street College Cafeteria, Mika Sneddon, Eliza Reed of Wave Hill, Peter Concannon, Lydia and Andrew Devine, Mitch Miller and the Rochester Philharmonic Orchestra, Desmond Maxwell, Ruth Hoffman, Jamie Tate, Gerry Gilfedder of Delta Hair Stylists, Tommy Zipser, Georgia Warner, Chuck and Maggie Close, and Hannah Spector.

Library of Congress Cataloging-in-Publication Data

Miller, Margaret (date)
Who uses this? / Margaret Miller.
    p.   cm.
Summary: Brief text, in question and answer form,
and accompanying photographs introduce a variety
of objects, their purpose, and who uses them.
ISBN 0-688-08278-5. ISBN 0-688-08279-3 (lib. bdg.)
1. Tools—Miscellanea—Juvenile literature.
2. Occupations—Miscellanea—Juvenile literature.
[1. Tools.   2. Occupations.   3. Questions and
answers.]
I. Title. TT153.M48   1990
331.7'02—dc20   89-30456   CIP   AC

For my father,
with admiration and love

Who uses this?

Carpenter

Who uses this?

Juggler

Who uses this?

Football player

Who uses this?

Baker

Who uses this?

Gardener

Who uses this?

Dog walker

Who uses this?

Conductor

Who uses this?

Barber

Who uses this?

Artist

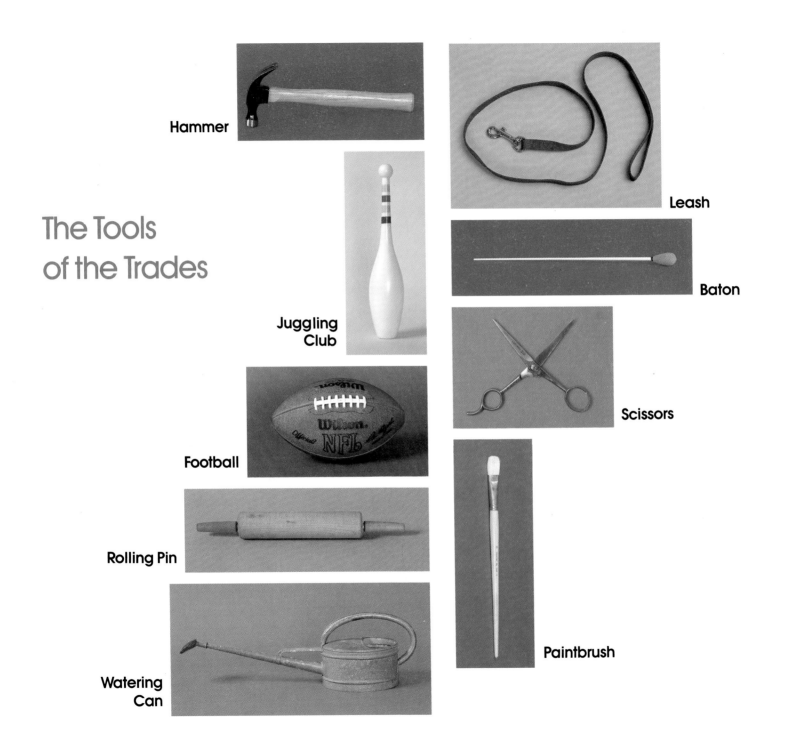

The Tools
of the Trades

Hammer

Leash

Juggling
Club

Baton

Scissors

Football

Rolling Pin

Paintbrush

Watering
Can